MY CHRISTMAS STAR

A Hide-and-Seek Story

By Sarah Reid Chisholm
Illustrated by Michelle Neavill

Augsburg
MINNEAPOLIS

For my star,
Holly

MY CHRISTMAS STAR
A Hide-and-Seek Story

ISBN 0-8066-2600-3   LCCN 93-70324

Manufactured in the U.S.A.   AF 9-2600

97 96 95 94 93 1 2 3 4 5 6 7 8 9 10

"When they saw the star,
they were overjoyed."
Matthew 2:10 NIV

The day I tried out for our church's Christmas play, Grandpa gave me a glow-in-the-dark star.

"Do your best," Grandpa said.

I got the biggest speaking part—the shepherd boy. That's the part I wanted.

When we came home, Mom said she was going to play a game with my star.
"I will hide it every day until Christmas. See if you can find it."

That night the star glowed on our Christmas tree. I didn't see it until Mom turned off the lights in the living room.

The next day I looked and hunted. Harry helped me find the star. Harry is my hamster.

Mom made a big mistake when she hid the star in the garage. I found the new baseball glove she bought me for Christmas.

I had to pick up my room the day my cousins were coming over. It took me all morning.

"This room is such a mess, you couldn't find anything in here," Mom groaned.

But I found my star!

One day we brought
Grandpa some cookies
shaped like stars. They
looked just like mine.

The next day I lost my second tooth. But I didn't lose my star!

Mom made me buy a Christmas present for my sister—even though she pinched me and let Harry out of his cage. I had to spend my last fifty cents on her.

At church we learned that the Wise Men followed a special star to Jesus. That star must have *really* glowed in the dark!

We sang songs one night at a home where my great-grandma lives. I was surprised to see where the star was hanging. I laughed all the way through "Silent Night."

Three days before Christmas it snowed. I had a snowball fight with my friends.

I didn't find the star until Mom sent me back outside to look.

My throat started to hurt a little that day.

The big night came: the night of the church play. I had a cold and couldn't talk—no voice at all.

Jimmie Strong got my part.

All I did was walk on stage and sit by the fire. I had to wear a sheep costume.

That was a rotten night. I was supposed to be the star, not Jimmie.

I spent all the next day in bed. Mom didn't forget to hide the star, though.

That night she came in to kiss me good night.

Hundreds of stars shone in the sky outside my window. God knows how many are up there. That's what Mom told me.

"You're my star," she said as she closed my door.

I'm glad God gave me a fun mom.

THE END